This Little Tiger book
belongs to:

_____

_____

_____

To Uli and Christian,
for whom this story was written ~ A S & B R

For Claire & Ari,
sisters in, and out, of law ~ S J

LITTLE TIGER PRESS
1 The Coda Centre, 189 Munster Road, London SW6 6AW
www.littletiger.co.uk

First published in Great Britain 2016
This edition published 2017
Text copyright © Andrea Schomburg & Barbara Röttgen 2016
Illustrations copyright © Sean Julian 2016
Andrea Schomburg, Barbara Röttgen and Sean Julian
have asserted their rights to be identified as the authors and illustrator
of this work under the Copyright, Designs and Patents Act, 1988
A CIP catalogue record for this book is available from the British Library
All rights reserved
ISBN 978-1-84869-270-1
Printed in China
LTP/1400/1653/0217
1 2 3 4 5 6 7 8 9 10

Andrea Schomburg & Barbara Röttgen

A Friend Like You

Illustrated by *Sean Julian*

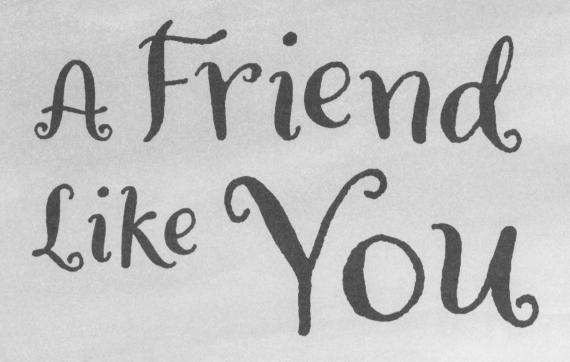

LITTLE TIGER PRESS
London

Once more, autumn had come.
Squirrel had been very busy, dashing
up and down the trees. And everywhere
he had buried nuts for the cold
months ahead.

When he was finished,
he sat down to rest.

"Aaaah," he sighed happily.
"All set for the winter."

Suddenly, a bird flew down
and landed next to him.

"Where did you come from?"
asked Squirrel.

"A long way from here," said the bird.
"And now I'm tired."

"Have a nut!" said Squirrel.

"Thank you very much!" replied the bird.
"But actually, I only eat worms.
More's the pity."

"Why not eat a nut for a change?"
said Squirrel.

"Hmmm, I might give it a try,"
answered the bird,
        tasting the nut carefully.

Then he fluffed his feathers
and hopped from
foot to foot.

"Well I never!" he chirped.
"Who would have thought it?
Nuts are delicious!"

"Would you like to come
climbing?" asked Squirrel.
"I'll show you my
favourite tree."

"Actually, I can't really climb,"
said the bird.
"More's the pity."

"But you can fly, can't you?"
said Squirrel.

"That I can,"
replied the bird.

Squirrel darted to the
highest treetop, and
the bird flew with him –
high, high up.

Squirrel turned somersaults
while the bird sat in the top
branches of the tree. He sang
so sweetly, it gave Squirrel
happy goosebumps
all over his back.

"Come sing with me!"
called the bird.

"Actually, I can't really sing,"
said Squirrel.
"More's the pity."

"Why not hum along?"
suggested the bird.

"Well," said Squirrel,
   "I might give it a try!"

The bird sang, and Squirrel hummed along,
bouncing on the twigs with joy.

They capered
and climbed,

and jumped
and hopped,

and flew, and sprang,
and sang together
all day long.

Then they sat on the grass, eating,
and watching the sunset.

"It's good to be with you!"
said the bird.

"And with you!" nodded Squirrel.
"When you sing, it gives me happy goosebumps
all over my back. Fancy us meeting like that,
out of the blue, and having so much fun together!"

"Yes," agreed the bird, "I never thought
I would meet a friend like you."

"You know what?" said Squirrel. "I've buried so many nuts, more than enough for two. And there's such a lot of space in my nest. Wouldn't you like to stay with me?"

"Yes," replied the bird. "I would. Very much. But . . ."

". . . but I can't."

"Why ever not?"
cried Squirrel.

"It was wonderful to spend the day with you,"
said the bird. "But I'm a bird, see?

I can't eat nuts all the time –
I'd come to miss my worms.

And it makes me so happy to fly.
I can't stay. More's the pity."

"But wait!" exclaimed Squirrel.
"You could still eat worms –
and just have nuts
for a change."

"You could fly away whenever you like
and then come back again. There are so many
lovely things we could do together!"

The bird thought for a moment.
Then he smiled and said,
"I might give it a try!"

And that's how
Squirrel and the bird stayed together.

And it didn't matter at all that they
were really rather different.
Quite the contrary.
It was just exactly right
the way it was.

More wonderful stories to share with friends...

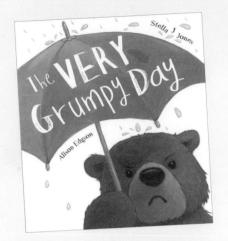

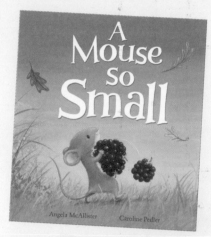

For information regarding any of the above titles or
for our catalogue, please contact us: Little Tiger Press,
1 The Coda Centre, 189 Munster Road, London SW6 6AW
Tel: 020 7385 6333 • E-mail: contact@littletiger.co.uk • www.littletiger.co.uk